THE UN-FORGOTTEN COAT

THE UN-FORGOTTEN COAT

Frank Cottrell Boyce

Photographs by
Carl Hunter and Clare Heney

CANDLEWICK PRESS

For Misheel

With thanks to Ben and Sarah at Full Circle Yurts; Sue Kendall; The
Brunswick Boys Club, Bootle; Anna McGrath for her coat; Caroline
Wheatley at Linacre Primary School, Bootle; Cheryl Mackie at SPACE;
Ermek Tleikhan, Batkhishig Luvsanpurev, and Tsogtgerel Namsraijav; and
Conor Lawrenson, Molly Lawrenson, Lewis O'Brien, and Shannonn Byrne.

Text copyright © 2011 by Frank Cottrell Boyce
Photographs copyright © 2011 by Carl Hunter and Clare Heney
Photograph on page 100 by Chay Heney

First U.S. edition 2011

Library of Congress Cataloging-in-Publication Data

Cottrell Boyce, Frank.
The unforgotten coat / Frank Cottrell Boyce ; photographs by Carl Hunter and Clare Heney. —1st U.S. ed.
p. cm.
Summary: When two Mongolian brothers inexplicably appear one morning in her sixth grade class, Julie,
who lives in a town near Liverpool named Bootle, becomes their new friend and "Good Guide," navigating
them through soccer, school uniforms, and British slang.

ISBN 978-0-7636-5729-1

1. Mongols—England—Juvenile fiction. [1. Mongols—England—Fiction.
2. Refugees—Fiction. 3. Emigration and immigration—Fiction. 4. Bootle (Sefton, England)—Fiction.
5. England—Fiction.] I. Hunter, Carl, date, ill. II. Heney, Clare, ill.
III. Title.

PZ7.C82963Un 2011

[Fic]—dc22   2010048224

18 19 20 APS 10 9 8 7 6 5 4

Printed in Humen, Dongguan, China

This book was typeset in Godlike.

Candlewick Press
99 Dover Street
Somerville, Massachusetts 02144

visit us at www.candlewick.com

our good guide

I hadn't seen this photograph since the day it was taken, until now. Even so, I can tell you anything you want to know about it. The boy on the left is Shocky. The one on the right is Duncan, who used to come to school with cookies in his pocket. He's married now, inexplicably. The girl on the left is Mimi Toolan, and the one on the right is me.

At the moment the picture was taken, I was mostly wondering whether Mimi would ask me back to her house after school. Mimi's mother let her play with her makeup, which my mother definitely did not, even though I was mature and sophisticated.

I was also thinking *Oh. My. Days. Shocky has put his hand on my shoulder!* Once, just before Christmas, I had managed to manipulate Shocky into being my partner in a classroom activity. This should have resulted in a moment of physical contact because it was a trust game, only it turned out that Shocky was not to be trusted. And by the time this photograph was taken, Shocky had completed an unbroken run of two hundred thirty-seven days of failing to notice my existence.

How do I remember my thoughts so clearly? Because those were the only thoughts I had in the first two terms of Year Six:

1. Mimi, can I come back to your house?

2. Shocky, please notice me.

Also, this photograph was taken in the summer term of Year Six. And doesn't everyone remember everything about their last summer in elementary school? The sports day. The graduates' trip. The graduation photograph. The endless discussion of which school you were going to next, the promise to stay friends even though you were going to different schools. Everyone signing their names on everyone else's shirts on the last afternoon. And all the time, you had the feeling that day by day, inch by inch, a door was opening and sunshine was pouring in, and any day now you would be allowed out through that door, laughing and yelling so loud that you wouldn't even hear when it closed behind you, forever.

I can tell you when it was taken. It was the second week of the summer term. During morning break, Mimi spotted two kids—one big and one little, the big one holding the little one's hand—staring through the railings of the playground. The little one was wearing a furry hat, and they had identical coats. Crazy coats—long, with fur inside. But any coat would have looked crazy. The sun was beating down. The asphalt in the car park was melting. Everyone else was wearing T-shirts.

Mimi went over and said, "What are you two looking at?"

The big one put his finger to his lips, shushing her, and said, "Pay attention to your teacher." He pointed at Mrs. Spendlove, and the very minute he did, she blew the whistle for the end of break, like he knew she was going to do it.

When we were all lined up, somehow these two were standing right behind me. I was looking at the little one, who had his hat pulled down right over his eyes. It looked so uncomfortable; I wanted to fix it for him—but the big one put his hand under my chin and turned my head away. "Don't look at him," he said.

He was asking for a slap, quite honestly. But before I could do anything about that, Mrs. Spendlove was walking us into class. The two boys went straight to the back, and the little one made himself at home in what was supposedly my seat. I stood there, staring right at him, thinking he'd take a hint. But no.

Mrs. Spendlove said, "Everyone, I'd like you all to say a big hello to a new face in our class. A happy new face, I hope. This is Chingis."

Everyone said hello except me. I said, "What about the other one, Miss? What's he called?"

She hadn't noticed the little one until then. "Oh. Chingis," she said, "I'm afraid your little brother isn't in this class. He's in Miss Hoyle's class just along the corridor."

"No," said Chingis, "my little brother is in this class. Look, he's here next to me."

Everyone laughed except Mrs. Spendlove. "Sorry, sorry," she said. "I mean he *belongs* in Miss Hoyle's class." She was flapping her hands at the rest of us to be quiet, mortified because she thought we were laughing at him, and it was her fault. But I was standing next to him and I could see he hadn't made a mistake. He was digging in.

"Julie, would you show Chingis's brother to Miss Hoyle's class?"

I certainly would. For one thing, I wanted my seat back.

As soon as I stepped towards the little one, though, the big one put his hand up, right in my face, and said, "No."

"Excuse me?" said Mrs. Spendlove.

"He must stay with me. I am bound to take care of him. Protect him. I must stay with him."

"Well, it doesn't really work like that, Chingis. For one thing, once he's in Miss Hoyle's class, she'll protect him. And besides, he won't really need protecting because . . ."

He wasn't even listening. He just took out some pencils and stuff and settled down to do a bit of drawing.

Mrs. Spendlove opened up her laptop and poked around for a while. "Ah," she said, talking to the little one directly. "You need to go to a different class, Kub—" and started trying to sound out this unbelievable name, syllable by syllable. Before she got to the third syllable, Chingis looked up and said, "No," again.

"No." Just like that.

It was the second time he'd said no to her. Once might be a mistake. Twice was game on. Definitely. We were witnessing a struggle for power.

Mrs. Spendlove made the first play. "Excuse me?" she said again.

"Call him Nergui," he said. "It's easier." Which was definitely cheeky, telling Mrs. Spendlove what to do, telling her she wouldn't be up to the job of pronouncing someone's actual name.

Mrs. Spendlove slapped that down. "Well, that's not what I've got here," she said, and tried sounding out the long name again.

Chingis stood up.

She looked him in the eye.

He said, "Please."

Please was good. *Please* was some kind of stand-down. *Please* was definitely points to her.

She closed the laptop really, really slowly. "OK," she said. "Just for today, you can stay in this class, Nergui."

Chingis said, "Thank you," and sat back down. It looked like victory for Mrs. Spendlove. Except that somehow this kid had ended up with everything he wanted—his little brother was sitting next to him, being called by some unofficial name. Maybe Mrs. Spendlove sensed this. Maybe that's why she decided she had to push it.

"So, if you take your hat off, Nergui," she said, "we can all get started."

The kid didn't move, and neither did Chingis. They both just sat there with *What are you going to do about it?* faces. Pretending they didn't understand.

She tried again. "I'm afraid you have to take your hat off, Nergui."

"No," said Chingis.

Now everyone looked at Mrs. Spendlove.

"We can't have people wearing hats in class, Chingis."

Everyone looked at Chingis.

This was like watching high-tension tennis.

"It will be dangerous to take off my brother's hat."

"How can it be dangerous to take off his hat? Is his head not securely fastened to his neck?"

She got a laugh for that. The laugh gave her some edge.

"Not dangerous for him. Dangerous for you."

Mrs. Spendlove frowned. Was he threatening her?

"If I take off his hat," he continued, "maybe he will go insane and kill everyone."

He was definitely threatening her. Threatening all of us. With his little brother.

"Chingis . . ."

"When you need your eagle to be calm, what do you do?"

"I don't know." She looked around the class. Did anyone know? Why *would* anyone know?

"Of course," he said, "you cover its eyes with a hood. When you want the eagle to fly and kill, you take off the hood. My brother is my eagle. With his hood on, he is calm enough. Without his hood, I don't know what he will be like."

Year Six. We had been at school for six years, and until that moment I thought I had probably learned all I would ever need to learn. I knew how to figure out the volume of a cube. I knew who had painted the *Sunflowers*. I could tell you the history of Saint Lucia. I knew about lines of Tudors and lines of symmetry and the importance of eating five portions of fruit a day. But in all that time, I had never had a single lesson in eagle-calming. I had never even heard the subject mentioned. I'd had no idea that a person might need eagle-calming skills.

And in that moment, I felt my own ignorance spread suddenly out behind me like a pair of wings, and every single thing I didn't know was a feather on those wings. I could feel them tugging at the air, restless to be airborne.

I wanted to talk to the new boy. I wanted to talk about eagles. But Mimi seemed to regard the whole Chingis incident as a minor interruption in the ongoing global cosmetics conversation. Only the boys were interested. At lunchtime, dozens of them crowded around Chingis and Nergui, asking them if they really had eagles, and how big they were, and whether Chingis was a liar or not.

"Where d'you get eagles from, then? Eagles 'R' Us?"

"Everyone has eagles where I come from."

"Where's that, then?"

"Mongolia."

They poked and pestered little Nergui, who still had his hat pulled down, hiding his eyes. They kept telling him to make eagle noises. The kid—Nergui—huddled down in his coat, pulled his arms out of his sleeves, and crossed them over his chest. His sleeves were flapping loose, and he did fully look like a bird.

Then Chingis spotted me over their heads and shouted, "You. You must come and help me."

I didn't know what he expected me to do. But I was fully delighted to be asked. I slid past the boys and then turned on them. "All right," I said. "Move on. Haven't you seen a pair of Mongolian brothers before?"

"No."

"Well, you have now. So move on."

"As if they're Mongolian, anyway." It was Shocky. "Why would they come here from Mongolia? They're probably from Speke."

Everyone agreed that the brothers were probably from Speke, and then went back to playing footie.

"Please stand still," said Chingis. He moved me back a bit and pulled something out of his bag that looked like an old-fashioned radio. When he pressed a button, it made this whirring sound, the top half shot open, and a lens popped out.

I know now that it was a Polaroid camera. At the time I think I thought it was some kind of crazy, starey cuckoo clock.

"I need a picture," he said, "so I can remember which one you are. You are to be our Good Guide here. OK?"

Mimi had come over by this point—she could hear a camera being deployed at five hundred meters. We both did our loveliest smiles, and that would be when Shocky and Duncan came over and got into the picture. Almost as soon as Chingis had clicked the button, a strip of paper rolled out of the front of the camera. He peeled off some kind of label, then waved the paper around in the air, and there we all were. Caught forever. He wrote something on the photo, which I didn't see at the time.

I saw it for the first time today. He'd written, "our good guide."

"You will be our Good Guide," he said. "In Mongolia we are nomads. When we come to a new country, we need to find a Good Guide. You will be our Good Guide in this place. Agree?"

Of course I agreed. No one had ever asked me to

be anything before, definitely not anything involving a title. And that was when I stopped thinking about makeup, lips, and Shocky. That was when I started walking around the place thinking, *Hi, I'm the Good Guide.*

I really did want to be a Good Guide.

eagle hood coat.

*T*hat's not Nergui's coat in the picture. That's Chingis's coat. I saw that coat today for the first time since we all left. I'd heard that they were going to knock down the school this summer. As it was the last day of term and my last chance to take a look, I went over on my way back from work.

Mrs. Spendlove was still working there, incredibly, and she recognized me right away. Thirty-four years she's taught there. Imagine that. She let me go around with her while she collected her stuff and some souvenirs. The old store cupboards, the cloakroom, her classroom. And there at the back of our old classroom was a big blue plastic tub with **LOST PROPERTY** written on it. Mostly trainers and socks and a few books, a lockable Miffy diary, a couple of *In the Night Garden* lunch boxes. And the coat.

The unforgettable coat of Chingis Tuul.

I lifted it out and held it up at arm's length. I wish I could say it looked like a bird, but it was more like a big hairy bat, just hanging there. I went through the pockets, the way you do.

And that's how I found these pictures.

demon eat this.

I really did take my Good Guide duties seriously.
I took Chingis and Nergui to the dining hall every
lunchtime and made sure they could sit together—even
though I didn't buy lunch myself. I made sure they
knew what they had to bring for games and swimming.
I told them to lose their weird-looking coats and wear
something normal. And when it was our class assembly,
I lobbied for it to be "All about Mongolia," thinking
that Chingis would join in and maybe even be pleased.
But it didn't work out that way.

I brought in pictures and looked stuff up on
Wikipedia for the first time in my life. He did
nothing. Even on the day, he just stood there, looking
Mongolian, while I told the school all I had learned
about how Mongolia, a landlocked presidential republic
in Central Asia, was the most sparsely populated
country in the world, where a lot of the people were
still nomads who lived in big tents called yurts and
the men liked to hunt wolves with eagles. And how
there was a city there called Xanadu, which was the
fifth Great Khan's summer capital. It had fountains and
brooks and meadows and woods that were full of every

kind of wild beast, and the Khan went hunting with his eagles there. The palace itself was made of tightly woven bamboo so that it could be taken apart and moved. Inside, it was all painted with birds and animals and trees so that you couldn't really tell if you were inside or out.

When someone said, "Is it really like that where you come from?" Chingis said, "Yes. Nothing has changed."

"What did you come to Bootle for, then?"

When everyone sniggered, he just shrugged his shoulders and said, "We are nomads. We move around."

I didn't do all this out of the goodness of my heart. It was part of my plan: I wanted to be asked back to their house. I imagined it would be stuffed with silks, with a horse-head fiddle in one corner and a samovar bubbling in the other. I really had done my homework.

Thanks to my obsession with Mimi's makeup, I already knew a bit about getting yourself asked back to places. All you had to do was walk with someone until they were nearly home, then say, "Oh, is this where you live?" and if that wasn't enough, just say you needed to use the toilet. Once you were through the door, their mother usually asked you to stay.

This didn't work with Chingis and Nergui, though, for the simple reason that they seemed to

take a different route home every day. One day they'd
head left up Hawthorne Road, so the next day I'd
go that way and wait for them to catch up. I'd wait
for ages and then discover they'd gone off down the
avenue. So the next day I'd go that way, only to see
them turn around and walk back the way they had
come, heading straight past me. Sometimes they'd
disappear into the terraces. Sometimes they'd even
slide off into the back alleys.

I gave up trying to follow them, but whenever I
was out, I would look at the windows of the houses
and flats, wondering if one of them was theirs and
feeling certain that somewhere in the narrow streets or
tower blocks there was a room with the silks and the
samovar, like a secret gateway.

Somewhere in Bootle, Xanadu was buried like
treasure.

Then one day I went into Savedra's shop for a bag of
Monster Munch and a bottle of Sunny D, and there
they were, the two of them, standing in the doorway
looking at me. Chingis said, "Are they good?" pointing
at the Monster Munch. I offered him some and started
walking slowly towards my house.

Chingis crunched the Munch. "Yes, it is good.
You can give some to Nergui."

We walked along, with them dipping into my Monster Munch every couple of meters. I subtly changed course whenever they changed theirs. I chugged some Sunny D so I could be convincing when I asked to use the toilet. But somehow we ended up outside my house, not theirs.

"I need to use the toilet," said Chingis. "And so does Nergui. You have toilets?"

"Sure. Come in."

As soon as they came through the door, my mum asked if they wanted to stay for supper.

"Sure," said Chingis.

He and Nergui went up to the toilet. Mum asked me if I thought they'd like fish fingers. "Or is that against their religion?"

"I'm not sure what religion they are. They eat normal school lunch."

We heard the toilet flush, but the boys did not come down. We could hear them walking around upstairs, opening doors and even drawers.

"That's a bit much, you know. Doors are one thing, but I draw the line at drawers," Mum said.

She couldn't, in fact, draw the line, though, because Chingis walked into the kitchen and said, "Please, we need to bake something right away. You have flour?"

Something in his voice managed to infect Mum

with baking panic. Personally, I'd never heard of emergency baking before. But Mum was yanking a mixing bowl out of the cupboard like it was a fire extinguisher. Bags of flour, slabs of butter—she threw them onto the table like medical supplies.

"Yeast?" Chingis asked.

"Yeast? We don't have yeast!" she said.

It seemed that we might all be doomed by lack of yeast and that only Chingis could save us.

"It's OK," he said. "This time I'll do it without yeast. Stand back, please. And warm the oven."

Mum more or less ran to the oven, and Chingis started throwing stuff into the mixing bowl and bashing the dough about. Nergui stood there watching as though this was heart surgery and it was his heart in the mixing bowl.

It was only when I said, "What is it exactly that you're doing?" that things started to calm down.

"Yeah," said Mum. "What is it exactly that you're doing?"

"You have some raisins?" asked Chingis.

"Sure." She passed him a bag of raisins. He squeezed the dough into the shape of a little boy and added raisins for teeth and eyes.

"You know, if we're going to eat this, you should have washed your hands."

"This is not for eating. Not for *us* to eat, anyway. We need something else to eat. What do you have?"

Mum said that she was thinking of having fish fingers if it wasn't against their religion.

"There is a religion in this country that forbids fish fingers?" asked Chingis.

"No, I don't think so. I'll put them on. Do you want to phone your mother and tell her you're staying for supper?"

"No. We are nomads. She doesn't expect us to come home like children who are not nomads. Maybe we will be staying here for the night."

"Oh, will you, maybe?" said Mum. "Maybe you won't, either."

Chingis glanced at Nergui. Then he looked around the room, as if checking that no one was listening. Mum had this mirror near the back door next to the "See How I Grow" chart. Chingis went over, took the mirror off the wall and turned it face down on the table. Then he closed the blind.

"We are telling you something in secret," he said. He looked at Nergui again, and Nergui nodded. "My brother believes he is being chased by a certain demon."

"A demon?" said Mum. "In Bootle? Are you sure there's only one?"

"We have to take steps to save him. For instance, Nergui is not his name. We never speak his name. Nergui means 'no one,' so if the demon hears us speaking to Nergui, it thinks we are speaking to no one."

"Right," said Mum. "Well. Obviously. Don't know why I didn't think of it myself."

"Also, we take a different route home from school each night so that it can't easily find where we live."

"But it does know where you go to school?"

"Nergui saw it in school. Twice."

"So he has actually seen this demon, then?"

"Of course. Or how would he know it was following him? We are not people who are afraid for no reason."

"Course not. So what does it look like?"

"It's in disguise. It looks like an ordinary man."

"So . . . how do you know it's a demon?"

"Because it wants to make him vanish. It's a demon that makes things vanish."

"Right," said Mum.

"That's why we had to leave Mongolia. This demon was there. It wanted to make us vanish. So we had to leave. We walked along the railway track that led out of our country. We followed the railway for days and days. Until we came to here."

"There's a direct rail link from here to Mongolia? Really?"

"Not direct, no. We make many changes. We do it to confuse the demon. And now I have made this boy out of dough. If we leave him on your doorstep, then maybe if the demon has followed us, it can think that this is Nergui. And maybe it will vanish instead."

"Great plan," said Mum. "Now if you're going to eat fish fingers, go and wash your hands."

So they stayed for supper. Before they ate, they put the dough boy on the doorstep. While we were eating, we watched the door. We couldn't help it. The lights as the cars went by, the voices of passing people, they all seemed like demon-related activities to me.

A few weeks before, I had not known that there was any such thing as a portable bamboo palace. I hadn't even known there was such a person as Chingis Khan, who had been born with a clot of blood grasped in his fist and who had conquered nearly the entire world in hardly any time at all, sweeping over the steppe into Central Asia and right up to the very gates of Europe. I hadn't even known there was such a place as the steppe! The steppe that was flat as pavement but as wide as a sea, with nothing but grass and great bustards. Wide as a sea and I hadn't even known it was there. If there were seas of grass and woven palaces in this world, why

26

wouldn't there be demons, too? And why wouldn't
one of them be crouched on our doorstep on William
Morris Avenue right that minute, munching a boy
made of dough?

*   *   *

Chingis cleared the plates without being asked. Nergui stayed staring at the door, looking tense.

"I think that little fella wants his mother," said Mum.

"I'll see if it's safe," said Chingis.

He opened the door and looked down at the step. The dough boy had disappeared.

"Honestly," said Mum, "you could leave a bucket of nuclear waste on your doorstep around here and it would be gone in five minutes. They really will take anything."

"We can go home," said Chingis. "The demon has eaten the dough boy. It won't need to eat again tonight."

毛工. one pound.

I remember this one, too. One day, Mrs. Spendlove made this announcement that we were going to do an experiment the next day, and we were all supposed to bring in a little canister, like an old-fashioned plastic film canister. "You are bound to have one hanging around your house," she said. "We're going to make our own rockets."

But when the next day came, no one had brought one in. She seemed disappointed. "I wanted you all to do this yourselves," she said. "I've only got three, so I'm afraid you'll all have to watch instead."

Anyway, she did this experiment where she stuck an Alka-Seltzer to the inside of the lid of one of the canisters with Blu-Tack, then she poured some water in the canister, put the lid on, and turned it upside down. No one was that interested, until about two minutes later when the canister shot up to the ceiling and hit a lightbulb, spraying water everywhere. Suddenly everyone wanted a go, but Mrs. Spendlove made this big speech about how you only get out what you put in, and how since none of us had gone to the bother of finding a canister, we would all just have to copy out some diagrams about the expansion of gases and propulsion and stuff, instead of having fun.

As soon as morning break began, Chingis went to the quiet-corner benches and announced that he had film canisters, Blu-Tack, and Alka-Seltzer all available for a pound a set. He opened his bag. He must have had thirty plastic film canisters, a massive slab of Blu-Tack, and a large pack of Alka-Seltzer.

"You can buy from me your own small rocket," he said. "One film canister, one stick of Blu-Tack, and an Alka-Seltzer—a pound."

Everyone wanted one. People were pushing around him, handing over money.

I said, "You brought these in, but you didn't tell Mrs. Spendlove? Why?" I'd felt sorry for her.

He said, "Why would I use them in the lesson? Last night I collected all of these from neighbors to sell."

"You could have sold them to us *before* the lesson. Then everyone would have had one, and she would have been really happy."

"Before she showed how it works, no one wanted one. No one would pay a pound when they don't know what it does. Now Mrs. Spendlove explains, everyone wants one. Her lesson was good advertising."

"But you brought Blu-Tack and Alka-Seltzer as well as the canisters—how did you know?"

"Rockets were invented in Mongolia. Propulsion is in our blood."

A lad called Backy—he's a policeman now—said, "They're my canisters. You can't make me pay for my own canisters."

Apparently, the night before, Chingis had gone and knocked on every door in his block of flats—including Backy's—and asked if they had any film canisters.

"I give you the canister free," said Chingis. "Blu-Tack is free also. Just one pound for the Alka-Seltzer."

Poor old Backy went for that. Honestly, they didn't know they'd been cut in half until they tried to walk away. Chingis got little Nergui to help him count all the cash. Thirty-four quid they made, and all day the school was full of popping sounds and quietly fizzing puddles.

There is only so much Good Guiding you can do on an elementary school playground. Even though I really tried to spin it out, I'd pretty much pointed out every stone and weed by the end of the week. Mrs. Harrison was the lunch lady—she had the power to give you a Band-Aid if you cut yourself. The big red box held outdoor play equipment—you could take what you wanted, but you had to put it back when you were finished. (Mrs. Harrison was watching.) The numbers and squares painted on the floor were for playing hopscotch, but no one ever did, because no one really knew how. The quiet corner—a little ring of apple trees with the bench in the middle—had been made in memory of a boy who'd died just before we came to the school. Everyone said he was buried under the trees and there were bits of him in the apples—but it wasn't true; he was buried in a graveyard like everyone else.

Until Chingis came, I had mostly spent breaks with Mimi, walking up and down beside the railings, talking about the inevitable future success of our imaginary girl group, the Surfing Eskimos. Until I took on the Good Guide duties, I'd had no idea there was a small tribe of sad-looking Year Five lads who more or less lived in the clump of trees that had been planted to hide the trash cans. They spent their time playing on their Nintendo DS's and avoiding Shocky and Duncan. I'd had no idea that Mrs. Harrison spoke French because she came from the Congo. I hadn't known that you could find frogs in the big clump of nettles between the playground and the car park. And I hadn't known there were Hula-Hoops in the outdoor play box.

Chingis took one out and asked me what it was. I put it over my head and tried to spin it around my waist, but it just clattered straight onto the floor.

"Oh," he said, "it's a Hula-Hoop. You do it like this."

He took it off me, dropped it over his head, and barely moving his hips, made it spin like a blender. He could carry on walking and talking at the same time. Nergui too.

Mrs. Harrison laughed and said, "You don't often see boys doing that."

Chingis stood still. The hoop dropped to the floor. He looked around the playground. "This place is nearly nothing but girls. Where are the boys?"

"This is the red playground," I said. "It's for anyone. If you want to play football, you go on the blue playground. It's through there. . . . Nearly all the boys play football."

Chingis led Nergui through the little gap between the dining hall and the main building and I followed. The two of them stood there for the rest of break, watching the boys charging up and down the blue playground, yelling and pointing and chasing the ball.

Chingis said, "Does this have rules?"

"I think so," I said.

"You need to find them out. We need to play this."

"Right."

So the two of them came back to my house and made me explain the rules of football. I had to borrow a ball from next door, and in the end, I had to borrow the little boy, too. Jordan, he was called. He couldn't understand why they didn't know how to play.

I said, "They're from Mongolia."

"Even so, they must have footie. They have footie everywhere."

"Not in Mongolia."

"No," said Chingis. "Mongolia is just horses, horses, horses. If we want to play with a ball, we get on a horse first. If we want to throw something or shoot something, we get on a horse. If we want to hunt, we get on a horse. If we get married, we take the bride on a horse. Only exception is wrestling. Wrestling is on the ground."

Jordan had heard of countries that had floods and disease and war, but he'd never heard of anywhere so bad that it had no football. He was nearly in tears. He taught them skills, rules, and tricks, and after that they sat on the pavement and he taught them the entire history of Liverpool FC.

Chingis said, "In football, it is just as much talking as it is playing."

From then on, Chingis spent morning break trying to get me to talk to him about the offside rule, the transfer window, and the history of the Champions League. He didn't play, though. He made Nergui play and took me to watch him. He'd point to him running up and down, barging into people, and say, "On the ball, yes, he's a bit of a donkey, but off the ball, he's a real workhorse." Even when he was talking about football, he was still quite horsey in his thinking.

Any football word he used—*foul, penalty, you've got to be kidding, yes!*—he said with a strong Liverpool accent. I'd been hoping he would turn me into some kind of Mongolian princess, but instead he was turning into a Scouser. "See our kid?" he said, pointing at the field. "Can you even tell which one he is from here?"

"He's the one with his hat pulled down over his eyes."

"That means nothing. Know the best way to hide a needle in a haystack?"

"I don't think there is a best way. Once the needle is in the haystack, it's really hard to find. I think that's the point, really."

"What if you've got a metal detector?"

"Do demons have metal detectors?"

"Don't talk about demons. Don't even mention them. OK? The point is: he looks just like any other kid now." And he did look just like any other kid. "The best way to hide a needle in a haystack is to disguise the needle as a piece of hay."

The truth was, the boys weren't just learning English; they were hiding themselves *inside* English, burying themselves in footie and insults, swearing and buzz words. They were *learning* themselves ordinary. And in our school, ordinary boys did not hang out with girls. Soon they didn't need a Good Guide anymore, and I found myself back at the railings with Mimi, planning our future fame and deciding what to wear on Own Clothes Day.

Own Clothes Day was when you were allowed to wear what you liked to school as long as you gave money to charity. I think there'd been a tidal wave or an earthquake. I say you were allowed to wear whatever you liked. In fact, if you were a boy you were allowed to wear an Everton football jersey—and risk being bullied by Liverpool fans—or a Liverpool football jersey—and risk being bullied by Everton fans—or something other than a football jersey—and risk being beaten up by everyone. Girls were allowed to wear basically anything they liked as long as it was really, really short and involved a huge purse. For some reason, I decided to go in the boy next door's Everton jersey. I probably thought it was my chance to remind Chingis that I was the one who'd taught him about footie.

When I got to school, he was waiting with Nergui at the gate. The two of them were standing completely still. They were wearing their crazy coats again—the furry coats they'd worn on their first day. And they were both wearing hats with fur inside. They looked mighty.

Chingis looked at me in my Everton jersey. "Perfect."

I thought he was paying me a compliment. I said, "It's just a footie jersey. It's not even an official one. It's a rip-off, and it's not even a rip-off of this season's jersey."

"Please come with us."

He made me wait outside the boys' toilets while they went inside. A few minutes later, he came out carrying Nergui's coat. "You wear this," he said. "Nergui will have your football jersey."

In the girls' toilets, a million tiny hooks of static tried to cling on as I peeled myself out of the nylon Everton top. Then I stepped into Nergui's coat as if I was stepping into another country. The cuffs were frayed and worn—I imagined that was where the eagle used to perch. The corners of the pockets were packed with grit—probably sand from the Gobi Desert. I was half expecting to find the rest of the desert waiting for me when I opened the door. It wasn't.

Chingis was waiting for me, though. And after Nergui had disappeared back into the toilets with the football jersey, the two of us stood there in the corridor, letting people look at us. No one said anything bad. We looked too scary.

When Nergui came out, it was the first time I'd seen him without his hat. He had long hair.

I said, "Nergui! You've got long hair! You look like a girl!"

"He thinks if he looks like a girl, his demon won't recognize him."

Nergui said, "You look like a boy in there. Maybe my demon will take you."

It was the first time I'd heard him talk, too. He sounded just like any other boy in our school.

I just said, "Maybe."

Obviously I knew they'd only asked me to swap clothes to confuse their demon. Did I care about being used as demon bait? No, because by then I didn't believe in demons. Plus, wearing that fur coat made me one of a pair with Chingis, one of a pair of swaggering nomads with eagle-calming skills and strings of horses somewhere in the desert.

In the afternoon, Mrs. Spendlove asked Chingis to tell the class a little bit about the clothes we were wearing. I stood up and explained that they had to be thick and warm because it could get so cold on the steppe, even in the desert at night. Minus fifty. And even though they hadn't asked me, I told them about Chingis Khan—whom Chingis was named after, just like lots of

Mongolian boys. Because I knew all about him, I said how when he was dying, he asked to be buried in a secret place with no monument so that the whole of his empire could be his gravestone. After his friends had laid his body in the ground, they stampeded a thousand horses over it to churn up the soil and disguise his grave. Then they all rode home and killed one another so that no one would ever tell the secret.

"What about you, Chingis? What can you tell us about your country?" said Mrs. Spendlove. Thinking about it now, that may have been a pointed remark as I seemed to be doing all the talking.

He said, "Well, there's the desert. And then there are some oasis things in the desert, you know, with trees that look like giant flowers." I didn't know about them. "They're sort of magical. And we have mountains that are made of metal, and they are shiny in the sun." I didn't know about them, either. "And if you're in trouble, you can make a pile of stones and maybe put some horse's skull on it or a prayer flag, and walk around it three times clockwise, and that'll help. It's called an *ovoo*."

"How will that help?" someone asked.

"I'm not sure. If you see one that someone else has built, you should walk around that three times, too. I'll show you a photo if you like."

And he did. He had photos of the desert. Of the magical oasis with the flower-like trees. Of the pile of stones.

Talking about these things made school and
Hawthorne Road and all of Bootle feel temporary and
little, as though we were just passing through on our
way to some indescribable adventure.

I kept that feeling all the way home, through the
front door, and into the kitchen, where Mum looked up
from the washing machine and said, "What the hell do
you think you're wearing?"

"It was Own Clothes Day."

"And those are not your own clothes."

"They're Nergui's. We swapped."

"Julie, I'm not being held responsible for someone
else's coat. You take it around to their place right now."

"But I don't know where they live."

It took Mum two phone calls to find out what I'd been
burning to know for weeks—where did Chingis and
Nergui live? Where was Xanadu? Turns out it was up
on the tenth floor of Roberts Tower—the apartments
nearest the overpass.

"And we're going over there right now," she said.

She packed the coat into a big plastic bag and drove
me over to the tower. When we got there, though, she
decided she didn't like the look of the place—there
was a pile of rubble in the middle of the car park, like a
lookout tower, with two kids perched on top of it.

"I'm not leaving the car here with no one in it. They'd have it ransacked by the time we called the lift."

"That's all right. You stay with the car. I'll go in."

"I'm not letting you walk into that place on your own, either."

"So what are you going to do? Drive the car into the lift?"

"Maybe leave it till the morning after all."

"No. No, I'm happy to go in." I didn't wait for her answer. I was running into Xanadu.

The lift was working but smelly. As it clanked up to the tenth floor, I pulled the coat out of the bag and put it on. I walked up to the door, thinking, *This is it. Their mum will see me in it and ask me in.* "Come in and lounge about on the silks while the samovar is bubbling," she'll say. "Father, give us a tune on your horse-head fiddle."

I rang the bell. I heard it ringing somewhere inside the flat. There were some voices. A door opened. Or maybe closed. Then it all went quiet.

I waited.

Nothing.

Maybe some whispering.

I knew it wasn't polite to ring twice, but I wasn't going to walk away. I'd been searching for this place for weeks. I'd been longing for it for weeks. I rang the bell again.

Silence.

A tense holding-your-breath type of silence.

Again.

Nothing.

A deep, rasping growl behind me made me jump. For some reason, I was thinking of their demon. But it was the lift. The doors opened, and Mum stepped out.

I said, "I thought you were waiting in the car?"

"Of course I'm not waiting in the car. As if I'm going to leave my own daughter to her fate just so I can look after the car. Did you smell that lift? Dear me. Have you rung the doorbell?"

"Yes."

"Didn't they answer?"

"Not yet."

"So they're not in. So let's get back to the car."

"Shhh. Listen." We could hear hushed voices arguing and water running from a tap.

"So they're in but they don't want to answer the door. They're probably having their dinner. Leave it till tomorrow."

She'd already pressed the button for the lift to come back. I said, "Maybe the bell is broken," and I hammered on the door.

The voices stopped. The tap stopped. I hammered again.

Mum grabbed my hand. "Don't do that," she hissed.
"It's rude."

But there were footsteps in the hallway now and
someone pulled the door open. A woman . . .

She was not wearing the traditional jeweled
Mongolian headdress. She was not wrapped in silk.
She was not happy to see me. She didn't see me at all
to start with.

She looked at Mum.

Mum said, "I'm Julie's mother. A friend of your
Chingis. This is his coat." The woman didn't answer.
She just stared at Mum and then at me. As if she
was trying to work out the answer to a puzzle. I knew
she wasn't going to ask us in. She stood and watched
me as I struggled out of the coat. I got a glimpse of
the flat—the long, empty corridor, the bare lightbulb
at the far end, and, near the door, a line of bags and
suitcases, bulging and fastened, as if the family was
about to leave.

I tried to hand back the coat, but she didn't take
it. Instead, she covered her eyes with her hands, and
I realized she was crying. I stood there holding the coat
while she held her face. Then a door opened at the far
end of the corridor and suddenly Chingis was striding
towards me. He didn't say anything. He didn't look at
me. He just took the coat, threw it over his shoulder

with one hand, and took hold of his mother's elbow with the other. He steered her back into the flat, then slammed the door in my face.

I thought Mum would go on about how rude they were, or how she was sure the car had been stolen. But she didn't say a word all the way down in the lift and all the way home in the car. It was only when we were safely parked on William Morris Avenue that she said, "Well, what was that all about?"

I knew exactly what it was all about. I didn't know the details or the reasons. But I knew it was all about fear.

I didn't know why. But I knew that everyone in that house was afraid.

The next day, Chingis came to school in his coat again and didn't take it off even when it was time to go to class. When I said, "Hey, it's not Own Clothes Day anymore," he didn't even look at me.

When he sat down, Mrs. Spendlove also said, "Chingis, it's not Own Clothes Day anymore."

"Yeah, and these aren't me own clothes, are they?" said Chingis. "They're me granddad's, see what I'm saying?"

He was doing his pretending-not-to-understand thing again, but it wasn't really that convincing now he had a thick Liverpool accent. Mrs. Spendlove said, "Just step outside, go to the cloakroom, and hang the coat up."

Chingis slouched out of the room. Mrs. Spendlove rolled her eyes, and Shocky said something like, "What d'you expect? He is named after Chingis Khan."

I said, "And what do you know about Chingis Khan, then?"

"Yes," said Mrs. Spendlove. "And what do you know about Chingis Khan?"

He was supposed to say, "Nothing, Miss," but in fact he stood up and delivered this whole lecture. "Chingis Khan was born in eleven hundred and something. He had red hair. When he grew up, he conquered, and what for? All he was ever interested in was horses. He just went around conquering countries and killing loads of people so he could have more horses. Like, he'd capture a city, and they'd say, 'What d'you want to do with it?' And he'd be like, 'I know! Let's knock it down, and we'll have a bit more room for our horses.' Or someone would come to him who'd discovered a new country, and they'd be like, 'The people there have wings and they can read minds and they've got a city that floats in the air,' or something, and he'd be like, 'Have they got any horses? No? Can't be bothered then.'"

I said, "But they were nomads. Horses were very important. They needed horses to survive. And for status. People nowadays, they use their cars to show their status."

"So if Chingis was alive today," said Shocky, "it would be cars instead of horses. He'd kill everyone so he could grab their cars and then he'd pave the whole of Europe so he could drive wherever he wanted."

It was hard to believe that I was actually having any kind of conversation with Shocky, let alone one about the history of the Mongol Empire. Afterwards, Mimi put it like this: "He obviously fancies you—otherwise why would he look up all that stuff about horses or whatever?"

Mrs. Spendlove broke into the Great Mongolian History Debate to ask, "Where actually *is* Chingis? He was only supposed to go and hang up his coat. Duncan, go and get him."

So Duncan went to get him. But he'd already gone. His coat was hanging up in the cloakroom, but there was no sign of him. Mrs. Spendlove said we should just concentrate on the lesson and let him sulk if he wanted to.

"He's probably gone to kill someone and then have a drink out of his skull. That's what the original Chingis did—and they're still naming their kids after him! Imagine that. Imagine if Germans called their kids Adolf. And then imagine if people followed those kids home every night and taught them how to play football and swapped coats with them and everything." Shocky was bright red by the time he'd finished.

I said, "At least they're polite enough to talk to

people and not just ignore someone for an entire year!"

"Excuse me," said Mrs. Spendlove, "could you two old married people take your domestic disputes somewhere else?"

Married? What was she on about?

By lunchtime there was still no sign of Chingis, and when I looked on the blue playground, there was no sign of Nergui, either. No one else seemed that worried. Kids did ditch school quite a bit—and anyway, Chingis seemed like he could look after himself. Only I had seen those faces at the door the night before. I knew about the fear that was in their house.

So I went through the pockets of the coat. I was trying to help. I found two tiny plastic chairs and a table, like from a doll's house. I seemed to know them from somewhere, but I couldn't think where. There was also a rolled-up notebook, with all his Polaroids stuck inside like Top Trumps cards. I flicked through the Polaroids. I came across the one of the oasis in the Gobi Desert—the one with the strange flower-like trees. Under the trees was a table and two chairs, the same chairs and table I was holding in my hand. I looked at the photograph again. They weren't flower-like trees at all. They were just flowers. And I knew which flowers.

I took the pictures, the notebook, and the doll's furniture out to the clump of trees where the Lost Tribe of Year Five lived. There were long, skinny flowers growing between the trees. I put the doll's furniture in between them, then crouched down and squinted. It took me about two minutes to find a perfect match. I swear I even found the tiny imprints of the table legs in the soil.

The magical Mongolian oasis was behind the trash cans in our school yard.

The *ovoo* with the horse's skull—when I looked again—was the pile of rubble in the car park of Roberts Tower.

What other wonders of the world were actually in Bootle?

There was also a Polaroid of two railway lines striking out across a flat prairie. Probably this was the railway line they had followed by foot on the epic journey across the steppe and along the Silk Road when they were trying to escape from the terrible demon.

Either that or it was the Merseyrail to Southport, which runs behind our school.

I rolled up the notebook, put it back in the coat pocket, and sneaked out through the blue playground. It was the easiest way out. If anyone stopped you, you could say you were going after a stray football. I walked up to the station, stood on the platform, and peered down the track. It looked completely different from the photo—it was all houses and overpass—except that the rails were identical. So I started to follow them.

I had been crashing through the nettles and broken
bottles along the tracks for about five minutes when
I heard this strange high-pitched singing coming from
the rails. I looked behind me. There was a blob of bright
blue light hovering over the rails. A train was coming.
I didn't think about it. I ran back to the platform and
jumped on board the train.

For five minutes there was nothing outside the
window but more houses and the rest of the overpass.
Then something flashed in the sun. A mountain of
scrap metal, towering over the Seaforth dock, shining in
the hot afternoon sun. Metal mountains.

After that came the fields. I'd had no idea till then
how close our house was to cows and horses. How come
no one had ever mentioned it? Maybe no one knew.
Maybe I was discovering an unknown country that
everyone had missed, even though it was so nearby.

After the fields came the trees. I put the Polaroid of
the Mongolian forest up against the window as the train
clunked into Freshfield Station. They were the same
trees. Definitely.

So I got off. And I walked up the road and into the
trees. Someone went by with a dog and smiled at me.
Like it was fine for me to be there. A couple went past
with a stroller with massive wheels. They said hello,

too. Then it was just trees and dark, worrying shadows in among the trees, and sometimes scratching sounds, though I could usually tell that it was just birds. And once I saw a squirrel. I was off the road now, following a sandy path. Every now and then, there was a little white post with a number on it. Which made me feel like I was going the right way for something, though I didn't know what. . . .

Then, all of a sudden, Nergui was walking next to me.

I didn't see it happen. I just sort of felt someone there, and then I saw him from the corner of my eye. "Where's Chingis?" I asked.

"Just coming. How come you got here before us? We thought we'd have to wait all night for you to catch up."

"I caught the train."

"Oh."

"How did you know I was coming?"

"You're our Good Guide. It's your job."

We sat on a log and waited for Chingis.

Chingis didn't seem surprised to see me, either. "Which way now?" was all he said.

I was quite buzzed by the way they just expected me to be there, in a forest. No one else has ever expected me to just be there in a forest for them. I liked being the Good Guide, so I said, "This way," like I knew what I was doing, and carried on following the numbered posts. Although it looked like we were at the end of the world, I knew there was a train every fifteen minutes that would take us back to Bootle in twenty-three minutes.

The whole thing reminded me of when a dream gets weird and you're sort of scared, but you also somehow know that you could wake yourself up and you'd be in your own bed, so you carry on dreaming just a bit longer. And that's what we did. We carried on walking.

When we spotted a pile of logs and twigs up ahead, I pointed at them like I'd arranged for them to be there and said, "I thought you might want to make an *ovoo* or something."

"Yeah. Good idea."

So the three of us piled the wood up into a pyramid, and Nergui went off and found a long branch to stick in the top like a flagpole. We tied my school sweater to it for a flag—even though it was getting cold. Then Chingis opened his bag and pulled out a horse skull.

"Where did you get that?"

"From my granddad's horse."

"Right. Well, obviously *that* would be in your schoolbag."

He put the skull on top of the *ovoo*.

I said, "Are we going to walk around it now three times in a clockwise direction?"

"Yes," said Chingis. "Which way is clockwise?"

I showed them, but Nergui was unconvinced. "Anyway," he said, "it all depends on the clock, doesn't it?"

I pointed out that all clocks go the same way.

"Of course they do," said Chingis. "You are so stupid."

So we agreed that all clocks went the same way, but none of us could agree which way that was. Even I wasn't sure—we've only got a digital clock on our computer. So we went around what I thought was clockwise, and then we went the other way—just in case. And then Nergui started to worry that by going one way and then the other, we were undoing what we'd only just done.

I said, "We could make a fire, but it's illegal."

"I don't want to break the law," said Nergui.

"We could dance. Dancing's not illegal."

They both stared at me.

"You're supposed to light a fire and then dance around it."

They both stared at me even more.

Then Chingis said, "Let's move on, then, lads."

So we moved on. And I explained to them that you could build a mental *ovoo* in your head if you wanted, and put all your good memories on it and a mental flag on top.

The trees grew thinner, and then we came to a field. It might have been a cornfield—some kind of long grass, anyway. I said we definitely weren't supposed to walk through that. You could see that no one else ever had. But Chingis was dead keen. "It will fully baffle that demon," he said. "You walk next to me, and Nergui will walk behind me so it'll look like the tracks of two people, not three. It will throw him off completely."

We trudged through the waist-high grass. Frightened birds flew up around us, whistling and beeping like little fax machines. And the corn rustled like wrapping paper. Chingis pulled the Polaroid camera out of his bag and took a picture of the tracks.

I said, "Chingis, where did you get that camera?"

"Refugee Project Summer Holiday Party in St. Anne's, Overbury Street. Won it in the raffle."

"They had a bouncy castle, too," added Nergui.

So that was this summer here in Liverpool? So you didn't have that camera when you were in Mongolia? So none of your photos are actually of Mongolia? Are you even from Mongolia? But I didn't say any of that.

Chingis shook the Polaroid dry and showed it to me. The funny thing was, it looked like Mongolia, as though he could turn bits of Liverpool into bits of Mongolia just by pointing his camera at them.

We carried on making our way through the field until we came out the other side. Now it was just sand in front of us, all the way to the sky.

"The desert," said Nergui.

"We are back in the desert, where we belong," said Chingis.

I said, "I think this is the beach, to be honest."

"If it's the beach, where's the sea?"

"Over there, behind the dunes."

"Honestly, this is the desert. Welcome to our desert!" And he took another picture—and he turned the beach into the desert with his camera. He gave me this photo and the one of the cornfield.

I made the boys slog up the dunes. The wind was

throwing sand in our eyes, and that really sharp grass was cutting my legs. I didn't care—I just wanted to show them that the sea was there and that they were wrong.

But when we got to the top of the dunes, there was no sea. Nothing. Just miles and miles of sand and mud shining in the sun.

"See!" said Chingis. "The desert."

I said, "The tide is out."

"No tide goes that far out," said Chingis.

*　　*　　*

We scrambled down the other side of the dunes. They
started to walk straight out towards the horizon, but
the wind was blasting in now, and bit by bit we ended
up following the line of the dunes. I pointed out that
since the sand was wet and muddy and there were shells
and seaweed and even starfish, this was clearly the sea.

"So where's it gone, then?"

"Maybe it's vanished. Maybe your demon made
it vanish. That's what it does, isn't it? Make things
vanish."

"Will you stop talking about it? Don't you know it
can hear you when you talk about it? If it does get us,
it'll be your fault."

"If it does get you, I'll be fully surprised. Don't you
know it's not real? And people don't just vanish."

"A lot of people just vanish. Practically everyone we
know vanished. That's why we had to leave home—
because people kept vanishing."

It was windy on the beach, and I wished my sweater
wasn't being used as a prayer flag. There was no one
around, and nothing seemed to be moving. I said,
"Maybe we've already vanished. Maybe this is where
you come to when you vanish."

"You'll get used to vanishing," said Chingis, who
seemed to think he owned the whole beach.

I was worried that the tide would come back in without us noticing and sweep us all out to sea. Also, the wind was cold, even though Chingis said it wasn't cold and went on about how in Mongolia you knew when it was cold because there was frost and snow on the hump of your camel.

I led them back into the dunes, away from the wind and the possibility of sudden drowning. They never asked me where I was going or why. I was the guide, and they were following.

"The less we know," said Chingis, "the less the demon can find out from us."

There was a rough path made from logs laid out on the sand, with gorse and nettles growing up in between the wood and on either side of the path. And poking out of the gorse, there were one or two of the numbered wooden posts. Without saying anything, I followed them to the top of a high dune, where we stopped and looked down, and for a minute we didn't say anything, but they each grabbed one of my hands and squeezed. . . .

Down beneath us, sheltered from the wind, was a cluster of plump Mongolian yurts.

"How did you do this?" asked Nergui. "Are we home? Is this Mongolia?"

It definitely looked like Mongolia. I had no idea how I'd done it but didn't want to admit it. I just said, "Let's see."

The yurts were all empty and there was no sign of life, except that the tents themselves seemed to be breathing as the wind moved in and out of them.

"Why is there no one here?" said Nergui.

"Is it all right to go in one?" said Chingis.

I had no idea whether it was all right or not, though I told him of course it was.

So we did. Inside, the air was warm and still, like the air of a different country. There was some kind of bamboo matting on the floor and a huge pile of cushions in one corner. We spread them in a circle on the floor and I noticed a gas heater. It had an ignition button, so I turned it on and we clustered around it. The air started to smell of slightly toasted sand.

Nergui said, "Why have the people who lived here vanished?"

"I don't think they've vanished. I think they don't come here till summer break."

Chingis had found some kind of storm lantern hanging from the central post. He lit it using the heater and took it outside.

"Where is he going?" I asked.

"Shhh, watch."

Chingis set up the lantern on top of a log so that it threw a pool of light onto the side of the tent. Then he stood between the lantern and the tent and made shadows with his hands. Sitting inside looking at the shadows he was casting on the canvas, we saw amazing shapes and stories. Chingis reached out his arm so that it looked like a horse's neck stretched out across the canvas, whinnying and neighing. He made a demon shape out of some cardboard he had in his bag.

Nergui screamed and told me to go out and make him stop.

I said, "Don't be thick—the pretend demon is putting fear in the real demon's face."

"Oh yeah. I never thought of that."

When Chingis made a girl shape with some grass for hair and did kissing noises, Nergui laughed till I thought he'd hurt himself.

Then Chingis came back inside, and we all sat staring at the lantern. Someone's stomach started to complain. I was thinking, *These two are nomads. Are they going to use their nomad skills to get food and water for us? I don't think so.* In fact, we wouldn't even be warm if the stove didn't have an ignition button. In my bag I still had my lunch. I spread out the food—a packet of Lunchables, some Quavers, a Capri Sun, and a ham sandwich. The two of them just stared at it like these were the riches of Kublai Khan. Then I said, "Go ahead," and they dived on it. There was a bit of a discussion about how to share the Lunchables, but we worked it out in the end and then just lay there, not chewing, just letting the cheese dissolve in our mouths. We took turns with the Capri Sun. First we sucked the juice out, and then we sucked the air. The noise it made as the plastic collapsed was hilarious for a while. Then it was really quiet. Except for when Nergui said, "What's that?" every time a twig snapped or a pinecone fell outside.

I thought, *These two don't know anything about being on your own, and soon it'll be dark. Somehow I've come out here with two nomads, and they've put me in charge!*

I said, "Back in Mongolia they tell stories around the fire."

"Go on, then."

"OK. I'll tell you a ghost story. Unless you'd be scared."

"Scared?" Chingis laughed. "We wouldn't be scared, would we, Nergui?"

"Not ever," said Nergui, looking around. "Where do you think everyone has gone?"

"I don't know," I said, and started the story. "There was this old man, in Italy I think it was." I was telling them the only story I knew. "He was an undertaker—do you know what that is? He buried people. When they were dead. And he was also very greedy. He loved jewelry the most. Anyway, one day, someone brings him the body of an old lady to bury—"

"Exactly how scary is this story?" asked Nergui.

"Completely scary. Want me to stop?"

"No."

"So someone brings him the body of this old lady, and she has a fabulous ring on one hand—"

"How fabulous?"

"Rubies."

"They're unlucky."

"Diamonds."

"OK."

"So he decides it'd be a waste to bury the ring. He's going to try and steal it. Well, he tries to pull it off.

Won't come. He rubs her hands with soap. Nothing. Still can't get the ring off. But the more he can't get it off, the more he wants it. So what does he do in the end?"

"Cuts off her hand." Chingis smiled. "That's what I'd do."

"And that's what he does—cuts off her hand. Then he folds her arms so no one will see. Then he sells the ring and buys himself a nice new car. Of course it's very hard to get rid of a hand without someone finding it and making a fuss, so he hides it in the glove compartment of his car.

"Anyway, one night he's out driving in that nice new car, and he comes to a crossroads. And he sees someone at the crossroads, standing there in the rain. So—"

"Oh, he doesn't stop, does he? Never stop at a crossroads," said Nergui.

"Well, *he* doesn't know that. And it's raining really hard, and the person standing there is old. An old woman. So he feels sorry for her and stops. 'Do hop in,' he says. 'I'll take you where you want to go.'

"This old woman starts to climb in, but it is quite a high-up car and not that easy to get into, so the man very kindly says, 'Here, give me your hand.'

"And the old woman says"—I did this next bit in a spooky voice—"'You already have my hand. . . .'"

As soon as I said that, Nergui screamed and ran out towards the woods.

We ran after him. But outside the tent, everything had changed. The sun had dropped by now. Our shadows stretched out in front of us, like wriggling flags, and the whole landscape seemed to be glowing. Chingis just went charging off, yelling, crunching twigs, and scaring birds. I went after him, grabbed him, and put my hand over his mouth to shut him up.

"Listen. We can't see him. So we've got to listen."

We held our breath. We listened. There was a scuffling somewhere off to the left. I picked up the storm lantern Chingis had used for the shadow show earlier and lifted it over my head as we walked slowly towards the sound.

Eyes. Bright green luminous eyes staring into the light. They seemed to be floating in the air.

"The demon!" gasped Chingis.

"A fox," I said. I could see it trotting off into the long grass, its head and tail both pointing down.

A cry came from somewhere in the long, golden grass. Something was in there, making the grass wave, sending ripples of gold across the field.

I shouted, "Nergui, stay still. We're coming."

We trudged through the grass, but we couldn't see him.

"He's vanished," said Chingis.

"Of course he hasn't vanished. Nergui! Shout to us again!"

He shouted, but the voice seemed to come from nowhere. Or from everywhere.

"He's vanished. He's just a voice in the air."

Then a thought struck me. "Nergui, are you crouching down?"

"Yeah."

"Can you just stand up?"

And there he was, right in front of us.

"Idiot!" said Chingis.

I said, "Right, follow me." I could see the yellow of the gorse, and it led me to the little white numbered posts. I counted them down—13-12-11-10—leading us back towards the road. Chingis and Nergui never asked where we were going. They just followed. Followed me all the way to the station and onto the train. We got off at Bootle New Strand. And they followed me, still not asking questions, all the way to Roberts Tower, clockwise around the pile of rubble, in at the main door, and up in the lift. They just padded along behind me.

But then when I knocked on their door, Chingis exploded. "What!" he shouted as if he'd just woken up. "What're you doing? What've you brought us here for?"

"It's where you live. I can't look after you."

"You've cheated. You've cheated us. She's done us in. Nergui, quick . . ."

Nergui spat at me. He was crying and shivering. Chingis was pounding on the lift button. You could barely hear the lift clunking up the shaft over Chingis's shouting. Then the door of the flat opened, and he went quiet. His mother walked onto the landing. She didn't even look at me. She picked up Nergui and carried him inside.

The lift arrived. Its doors creaked open. Chingis stood there staring into it as if he might still step inside. His mother stood in the doorway watching him. Two doors. Two places to go. The lift doors began to close. Chingis turned around and walked through the lit door, into the flat.

When I stepped towards the lift, the doors started to reopen. I looked back at the flat to see if the boys would say anything. Ask me in maybe. But nothing. Their mother closed the door, and I stepped into the lift. The doors closed me in.

When I got home, I told my mum I'd been to Mimi's.

On the way to school the next day, I talked to Mimi about it. "They were idiots. They thought they could run away, but Chingis didn't even bring his coat. Hunting with eagles? They were scared of a fox. I saved their lives. They'd have died of hunger without me."

"What were they running away for, anyway?"

I didn't want to tell her about the demon because it was so stupid, so I just said, "I don't know."

"Maybe their mum is a bit of a witch. She never comes to get them, does she?"

"No. But honestly, they were on the beach and they didn't even know it was the beach. If the tide had come in, they would have drowned. I saved their lives."

"I don't know why you bothered. I don't know why you hang around with them, anyway."

"Well, I won't now."

Which I didn't.

*   *   *

Because during the first lesson Mrs. Spendlove came in and stood in front of the class without saying anything for ages. She did this so long that, in the end, everyone went quiet.

"I've got some very sad news," she said into the unexpected quietness. "I got a phone call today, in the very early hours of the morning. It was from Chingis."

Everyone sat up. *Who phones a teacher?*

"It's a complicated situation and I don't know all the details, but basically, because of things to do with the law, Chingis's family was not supposed to be in this country. They didn't have the right papers, and though they'd been trying to get them, they ran out of time. I'm afraid the police came very early this morning to take them away and send them back to their own country. That's why Chingis rang me. He wanted to say good-bye to you all."

And that was that. We never saw him again.

I thought about things, talked about things. Mostly with Shocky, funnily enough. He was the only one who seemed to grasp how bad this was.

I think Chingis knew that something was going to happen. Of course he did. Their bags were packed and in the hall. His mother was terrified when there was an unexpected knock on the door. He knew it was going to happen. They were going to come.

I think he had some idea that if he ran away with Nergui, then maybe when the police—or whoever—came, they wouldn't make their parents leave because the kids were missing. I think he thought that if he could hide out for a while, maybe it would be OK.

But I found him. The Good Guide. I took him home. And that's where they got him. I'd led him straight back to them.

The day Mrs. Spendlove made the announcement, I waited in the cloakroom after school, wondering what to do. I watched all the coats go one by one, until only one was left.

"Miss!" I shouted as she came out of the classroom. "Look, Chingis's coat. It's still here." How could his coat be here and not him? "They'll have to let him come back for his coat, Miss, won't they, Miss?"

"I'm not sure, Julie. No, I don't think so."

"But temperatures reach as low as minus fifty on the steppe in winter. There's frost on the humps of the camels, Miss. How can they send someone there without a coat?"

"Maybe someone will give him another one."

"It's a special coat, though, Miss—for extreme conditions. It's a traditional Mongolian coat."

"I'll take it. How about that? When we find out where they are, I'll send it to him."

"That'd be best, Miss. Can you do that?"

"I'll do it first thing."

But she left the coat hanging there when she went. And it was still there the next morning. And here it is now, all these years later, in the lost property box. It was never returned.

I can see now that it wasn't anything like a traditional Mongolian coat. It's some kind of big, ancient hippie coat. An Afghan coat. There's a label inside that says BIBA—LONDON. They probably got it from a charity shop or the box of donations at the refugee center.

And in the pocket are the photographs. Photographs of a Mongolia cobbled together from bits of Bootle. Chingis's Mongolia was one big mental *ovoo*.

"Did you ever hear from him again, Miss?"

"Call me Claire, now that you're a grown-up, Julie."

"Yes, Miss."

"No. I don't know how bad things were for them. It really was true that they'd walked out of Mongolia following the railway line. I don't suppose they did that because they were having fun."

"You don't happen to have any pictures of him, do you? All these photos, he took them himself, so he's not in any of them."

"No. I'm sorry."

That night I pick up my little one from the babysitter, take her home, feed her, and while she is busy with her Playmobil, I root out the Polaroids Chingis had given me that day on the beach and put them in his notebook with the others. In bed later, I flick through the notebook with her and make up a bit of a story to go with the photos, pretending it's a picture book. I examine every photo in case he appears in one of them. But no. How could he? He took them all himself.

Then, wedged in the middle, I find one Polaroid that's completely black. . . .

The black is the cover you pull off a Polaroid when
it's developed. So this one has never been exposed.
Maybe he took a picture of himself. I dig into the black
with my fingernails, and the cover starts to come up.
I can peel it off. So I do. . . .

Polaroids don't work like that, though. If you leave them too long, the light turns back into darkness. Polaroids are like people.

It's only when I close the notebook and see his name written in full on the front page that I realize I could just Google him.

*   *   *

It turns out that Tuul is the third most common surname in Mongolia, and every single boy is called Chingis. That's if his name really was Chingis. There were pages and pages of Chingis Tuuls. I'd also forgotten that I didn't read Mongolian. So there were pages and pages of strange-looking letters with his name highlighted every now and then. Maybe he's the president now or the winner of *Mongolia's Got Talent* or something.

Of course, Julie O'Connor is not an unusual name, either. If he was Googling me from Mongolia, what would he find? Pages and pages about a girl who runs a kayak school in California. A woman who makes coats to order in Cleveland. An aromatherapist in Newcastle. Even "Julie O'Connor + Liverpool" gives you a dieting blog, a barrister, two grief counselors, and street dance lessons. Even if you just search Facebook there are more than two dozen of us, with only our profile pictures to identify us. And I'm sure none of us look like we did when we were eleven.

And, anyway, why would he be looking for me? He probably still thinks it was my fault he got deported.

I scan the Polaroids and add them to my Facebook page. I even change my profile picture to that photo of the coat hanging in the cloakroom.

Two days later, he requests me as a friend. Maybe it was a coincidence. Maybe he's been checking all the Julie O'Connors in the world every day for years. I don't know. But he's asked to add me. So I accept the request, say thanks, and ask if he wants the coat back.

He puts "yes, please" and messages me his address. And he tags me in this photograph:

Julie, you were
our good guide
and friend.
Thank you.
Love chingis and Nergui.
x x x x x

Afterword

A few years back, just after my book *Millions* came out, a teacher asked me to come and visit her elementary school. The teacher's name was Sue Kendall, and the school was Joan of Arc Primary in Bootle. It was my very first author visit—the first time I'd ever heard myself described as an author, the first time I'd ever strolled into an unfamiliar building and had a bunch of strangers sit in a circle and listen while I told a story. Amazing. I felt like Homer.

I've done it hundreds of times since, but it still feels full of ancient magic to me. And I remember pretty much every detail of that first time. There was a big boy there called Christian, who was one of the inspirations for the overgrown Liam in my book *Cosmic*. Mrs. Kendall and Joan of Arc Primary are always popping up in my stories. But the thing I remember most is meeting a girl called Misheel. She was a refugee from Mongolia, and she just lit up the room. The other children were touchingly proud of her and told me about the time Misheel showed up to the school dance in full Mongolian costume with her elaborate headdress and fabulous robes. They knew all about Mongolia—its customs and epic landscape—because of her. Her presence massively enriched their lives. Everyone must have felt the same way, because she was chosen to lead the Lord Mayor's procession that year.

There's a line in this book about Xanadu being hidden in the heart of Bootle, and that's what she seemed to be—a wonder of the world living among them.

Then one day the Immigration Authorities came and snatched her and her family in the middle of the night. Misheel managed to get one call through to Sue Kendall before one of the officers grabbed her phone. And, of course, she has not been seen since. I don't know much about immigration policy or the politics of the U.K.'s relationship with Mongolia. Maybe there is some complicated reason why a depopulated and culturally deprived area like Bootle shouldn't be allowed generous and brilliant visitors. I do know that a country that authorizes its functionaries to snatch children from their beds in the middle of the night can't really be called civilized.

The Joan of Arc children were upset, of course, and one of the things that most worried them was that Misheel had left her coat behind. They knew that it was cold in Mongolia and worried about how she would manage without it. That image of the left-behind coat really haunted me. I talked to my friends Carl Hunter and Clare Heney at the time, and we planned to make a documentary in which we took some of the kids to Mongolia to look for Misheel and give her back her coat. But it never happened.

Then last year, Jane Davis asked me to write a book for Our Read. I went to meet her with a pocketful of stories—stories about the Gold Rush, about the future, about ghosts—all of them thought out and ready to go, but somehow I found myself talking about Misheel instead. I said, "But actually that's not a story, that's just something that happened." But we both knew that this was the story I really wanted to write. And that Carl and Clare should be working on it with me.

I changed Misheel into a boy for this book. Because this isn't Misheel's story. It's a made-up story. I didn't want to tell Misheel's story because I didn't want that story to be over. Strangely, as I was putting the finishing touches on this book, I bumped into Sue Kendall and she told me that Misheel had—for the first time ever—rung her that morning from Mongolia. I wanted to know everything that had happened to her. But that really is a different story.

Frank Cottrell Boyce

Carl, Clare, and Frank

Frank Cottrell Boyce won the 2004 Carnegie Medal for his first children's book, *Millions.* He has since written numerous other books for children, including a trilogy of sequels to Ian Fleming's classic *Chitty Chitty Bang Bang*— *Chitty Chitty Bang Bang Flies Again, Chitty Chitty Bang Bang and the Race Against Time,* and *Chitty Chitty Bang Bang Over the Moon*—all illustrated by Joe Berger. Frank Cottrell Boyce is also an accomplished and successful screenwriter and wrote the opening ceremonies for the 2012 Olympic Games in London. He lives with his family in Liverpool.

Carl Hunter is a filmmaker and also plays bass guitar for Liverpool-based band The Farm. **Clare Heney** is a filmmaker and photographer. She and Carl both lecture in media at Edge Hill University.

Together, the trio has collaborated on a number of projects, including the film *Accelerate.*

Frank Cottrell Boyce wrote *The Unforgotten Coat* to support the Reader Organisation, helping them in their aim to bring about a reading revolution.

The Reader Organisation is a pioneering charity, working across the U.K. and beyond, making it possible for people of all ages, backgrounds, and abilities to enjoy and engage with reading. The work they do is driven by a love for great literature and a strong belief that shared reading is a deeply powerful activity that can significantly enrich and improve lives and the communities we live in.

Through their hundreds of Get into Reading groups, Read to Lead training, Our Read campaign, and Community Theatre and Reader-in-Residence projects in hospitals, care homes, prisons, schools, and libraries, the Reader Organisation is transforming society's collective approach to reading by making literature accessible, available, emotionally rewarding, and fun.

This book is part of the reading revolution! Please go out there and share it with someone you know.

Visit www.thereader.org.uk to learn more.

31901064557392